Leabharlann nan Eilean

D1390399

J39852130

AHLBERG

- 1 SEP 2009

WITHDRAWN

WESTERN ISLES
LIBRARIES
J39852130

The Black Cat

ALLAN AHLBERG · ANDRE AMSTUTZ

MAMMOTH

In a dark dark town,
on a cold cold night,
under a starry starry sky,
down a slippery slippery slope,
on a bumpety bumpety sledge . . .

a little skeleton is sliding . . .
and sliding . . .
and crashing – wallop!

The little skeleton
loses a leg in the snow.
A white leg in snow
is hard to find.
A black cat in snow
is easy to find.
What is <u>she</u> doing here?

The little skeleton and the big skeleton
go to the bone-yard
to get a new leg
for the little skeleton.

They play around with the bones
for a while . . .
and go home to bed.

Then . . .
in the dark dark town,
on <u>another</u> cold cold night,
under a starry starry sky,
down a slippery slippery slope,
on a bumpety bumpety sledge . . .

two skeletons are sliding . . .
and sliding . . .
and sliding . . .
and crashing – bang!
WALLOP!
This time the big skeleton
loses a leg in the snow.

CRASH

A white leg in snow
is hard to find.
A black cat is easy.
Is she still here?
I wonder why.

The big skeleton
and the little skeleton
go to the bone-yard
to get a new leg
for the big skeleton.

They play around again with the bones
and go home to bed.

Then . . .
in the dark town,
on the <u>next</u> night,
under a starry sky,
with a moon, too,
down a slippery slope,
in the frosty air,
on a bumpety sledge . . .

three skeletons are sliding . . .
and sliding . . .
and shouting . . .
and barking!
And banging! Wallop!

CRASH!

This time the big skeleton
and the little skeleton
lose the dog skeleton.
A white dog in snow
is hard to find.
But a noisy dog is easy to find.
So is a black cat!

The dog skeleton chases the cat.
Now we know –
that's what she is here for!

The dog chases the cat
up and down
the dark dark hill,
in and out
of the dark dark bone-yard,

round and round
the dark dark streets
and down and down
to the dark dark cellar.

But a black cat in a cellar
is very hard to find.
Can <u>you</u> see her?

Well, the dog skeleton couldn't,
and the little skeleton couldn't,
and the big skeleton didn't even try.
So off they went – at last – to bed.

Meanwhile . . .
in the same town,
on the same night,
under the same sky,
down the same slope,
a bumpety sledge is sliding . . .

with a black cat on it.

First published in Great Britain 1990
by William Heinemann Ltd
Published 1992 by Mammoth
an imprint of Reed Consumer Books Ltd
Michelin House, 81 Fulham Road, London SW3 6RB
and Auckland, Melbourne, Singapore and Toronto

Reprinted 1992 (four times), 1993 (twice), 1994 (twice), 1995, 1996

Text copyright © Allan Ahlberg 1990
Illustrations copyright © André Amstutz 1990

The right of Allan Ahlberg and André Amstutz to be identified as
author and illustrator of this work has been asserted by them in
accordance with the Copyright, Designs and Patents Act 1988

ISBN 0 7497 1040 3

A CIP catalogue record for this title
is available from the British Library

Printed in Great Britain
by Scotprint Ltd, Musselburgh

This paperback is sold subject to the condition
that it shall not, by way of trade or otherwise,
be lent, resold, hired out, or otherwise circulated
without the publisher's prior consent in any form
of binding or cover other than that in which
it is published and without a similar condition
including this condition being imposed
on the subsequent purchaser.